For teachers and librarians everywhere.—L.N. & F.B.

If You Take a Mouse to School

If You Take a

BY **Laura Numeroff**

ILLUSTRATED BY **Felicia Bond**

Laura Geringer Books
An Imprint of HarperCollins*Publishers*

If You Take a Mouse to School
Text copyright © 2002 by Laura Numeroff
Illustrations copyright © 2002 by Felicia Bond
For information address HarperCollins Children's Books, a division of
HarperCollins Publishers, 10 East 53rd Street, New York, NY 10022.
Manufactured in China. All rights reserved.
www.harperchildrens.com
Library of Congress Cataloging-in-Publication Data
Numeroff, Laura Joffe.
   If you take a mouse to school / by Laura Numeroff ; illustrated by Felicia Bond.
      p.   cm.
   Summary: Follows a boy and his mouse through a busy day at school.
   ISBN: 978-0-06-212870-6
   [1. Schools—Fiction.   2. Mice—Fiction.]   I. Bond, Felicia, ill.   II. Title.
PZ7.N964Ii   2002   00-067280
[E]—dc21   CIP
                                                                                AC

           12 13 14 15 16 LEO 10 9 8 7 6 5 4 3 2 1

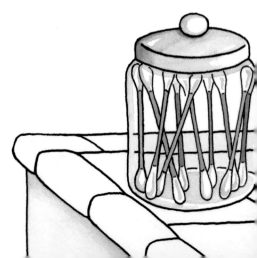

Mouse to School

If you take a mouse to school,

he'll ask you for your lunchbox.

When you give him your lunchbox,
he'll want a sandwich—

and a snack for later.
Then he'll need a notebook
and some pencils.

He'll probably want to share your backpack, too.

When you get to school,
he'll put his things
in your locker
and take a look around.

He might do a little math,

and spell a word or two.

He'll even try a science experiment!

Then he'll need to wash up.

You'll have to take him to the bathroom.

Once he's nice and clean,

he'll be ready for his lunch.

On the way to the lunchroom,
he'll see some building blocks.

He'll build a little mouse house

and make some furniture out of clay.

Then he'll need some books
for his bookshelf.
He'll start by writing
one of his own,
so he'll need a lot of paper.

He'll probably use up all
your pencils.

When he's finished,

he'll want to read his book to you.

Then he'll want to take it home.
So he'll put it in your lunchbox,

and tuck it in a safe place.

When the bell rings,
he'll run out to wait for the bus.

While he's waiting,
he'll play a quick game of soccer.

Then he'll ask you to
shoot a few baskets,

and do a little skateboarding.

When he stops to catch his breath,
he'll want to eat his snack.

So he'll ask you for your . . .

lunchbox.

And chances are,

if he asks you for your lunchbox,

you'll have to take him

back to school.